To Andrew
Goldstein.

andrew@cmgoldstein
.com

Scooby-Doo!™
The Mystery Mansion

By Annie Auerbach

ABDO Spotlight

ABDOPUBLISHING.COM

Reinforced library bound edition published in 2016 by Spotlight, a division of ABDO
PO Box 398166, Minneapolis, Minnesota 55439. Spotlight produces high-quality
reinforced library bound editions for schools and libraries. Published by agreement
with Warner Bros. Entertainment Inc.

Printed in the United States of America, North Mankato, Minnesota.
092015
012016

THIS BOOK CONTAINS
RECYCLED MATERIALS

CATALOGING-IN-PUBLICATION DATA

Auerbach, Annie.
 Scooby-Doo in the mystery mansion / Annie Auerbach.
  p. cm. (Scooby-Doo)
 Summary: A mysterious masked figure is ruining business at a hotel mansion. Can Mystery, Inc.
catch the masked figure before it's too late?
 1. Scooby-Doo (Fictitious character)--Juvenile fiction. 2. Dogs--Juvenile fiction. 3. Mystery and
detective stories--Juvenile fiction. 4. Adventure and adventures--Juvenile fiction.
 [E]--dc23
                           2015156073

 978-1-61479-411-0   (Reinforced Library Bound Edition)

Spotlight
A Division of ABDO
abdopublishing.com

The Mystery Machine cruised down the road. The gang was heading toward a campsite on the beach. Above the ocean, they could see dark clouds.

"Uh-oh," said Daphne, looking out the window. "I hope those clouds aren't heading our way."

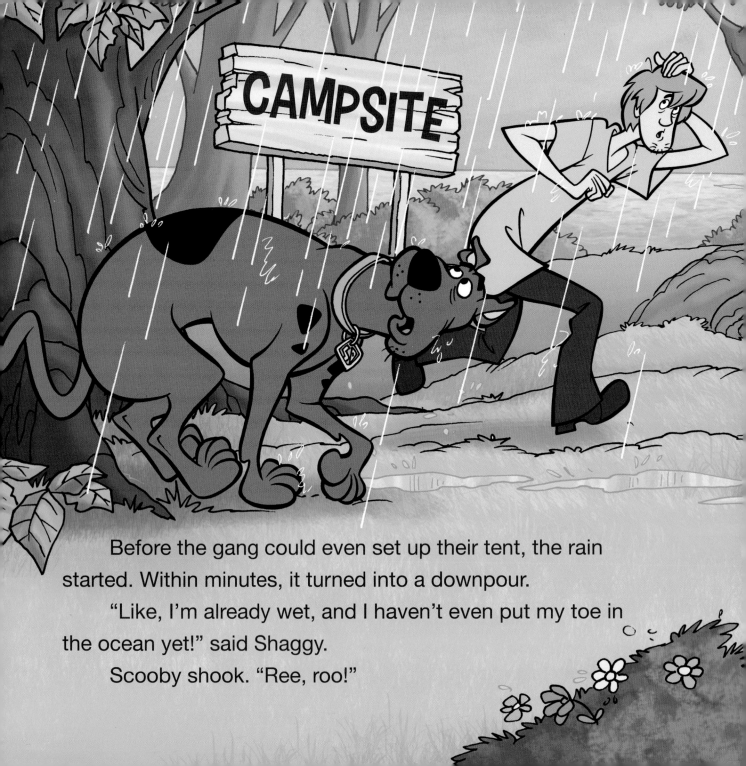

Before the gang could even set up their tent, the rain started. Within minutes, it turned into a downpour.

"Like, I'm already wet, and I haven't even put my toe in the ocean yet!" said Shaggy.

Scooby shook. "Ree, roo!"

"I guess we'll have to cut this camping trip short—very short," said Fred.

Everyone piled back into the van and looked for someplace to stay for the night.

Before long, they came upon a hotel mansion high on a cliff.

Fred turned into the driveway.

"Let's see if they have any rooms available," he said.

As soon as the gang walked in, the owner of the hotel rushed over and introduced himself. "Welcome! Welcome!" he said. "I am Mr. MacDuff. I'm so pleased to have you stay with us." He went on to explain that the hotel had been family-run for over 100 years. "But business has been so slow lately, I'm not sure how much longer we can stay open."

"That's too bad," said Velma.

Just then, Mr. MacDuff called to the bellhop and handed him some keys. "Marty, will you show these folks to their rooms?"

Marty nodded. He led them upstairs and then said, "Wow, you guys are brave."

"Brave? Why?" asked Fred.

"Well, this place is haunted," explained Marty. "That's why no one stays here anymore."

"Zoinks!" said Shaggy. "Maybe we shouldn't stay here either!"

"Don't be silly," said Fred. "Besides, in this weather, there's nowhere else to go."

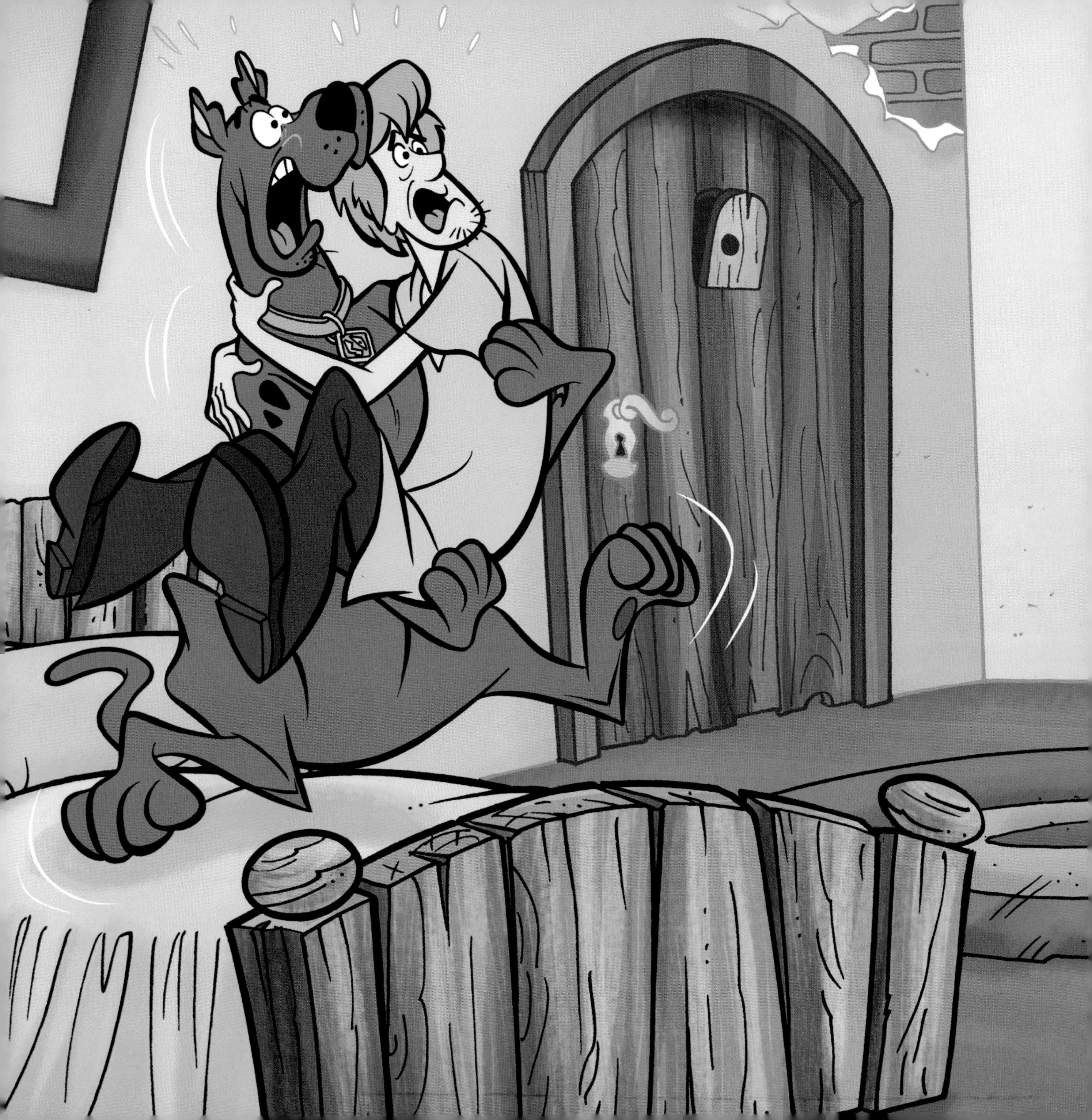

Just after midnight, Shaggy, Scooby, and Fred were woken up by some strange noises and scary voices.

"Get out! Get out before it's too late!"

"Like, is it just me, or is someone trying to tell us something?" said Shaggy. "Maybe it's time to go."

The guys ran into Daphne and Velma in the hall, who had heard the same thing.

"Let's go investigate," said Fred.

"I was afraid you'd say that," Shaggy said.

"We'll split up," suggested Fred.

"I was afraid you were gonna say that, too," said Shaggy.

"You guys check up here, and the rest of us will look downstairs," Fred said.

Shaggy gulped. "Come on, Scoob," he said. "Let's start looking. But I really, really, really hope we don't find anything!"

"Re, roo," agreed Scooby as he followed Shaggy down the hall.

The first two rooms were empty. But Scooby and Shaggy heard a terrible moaning coming from the third room. Just then the door opened and a masked figure lunged for them.

"Zoinks!"

Shaggy and Scooby ran to the end of the hall.

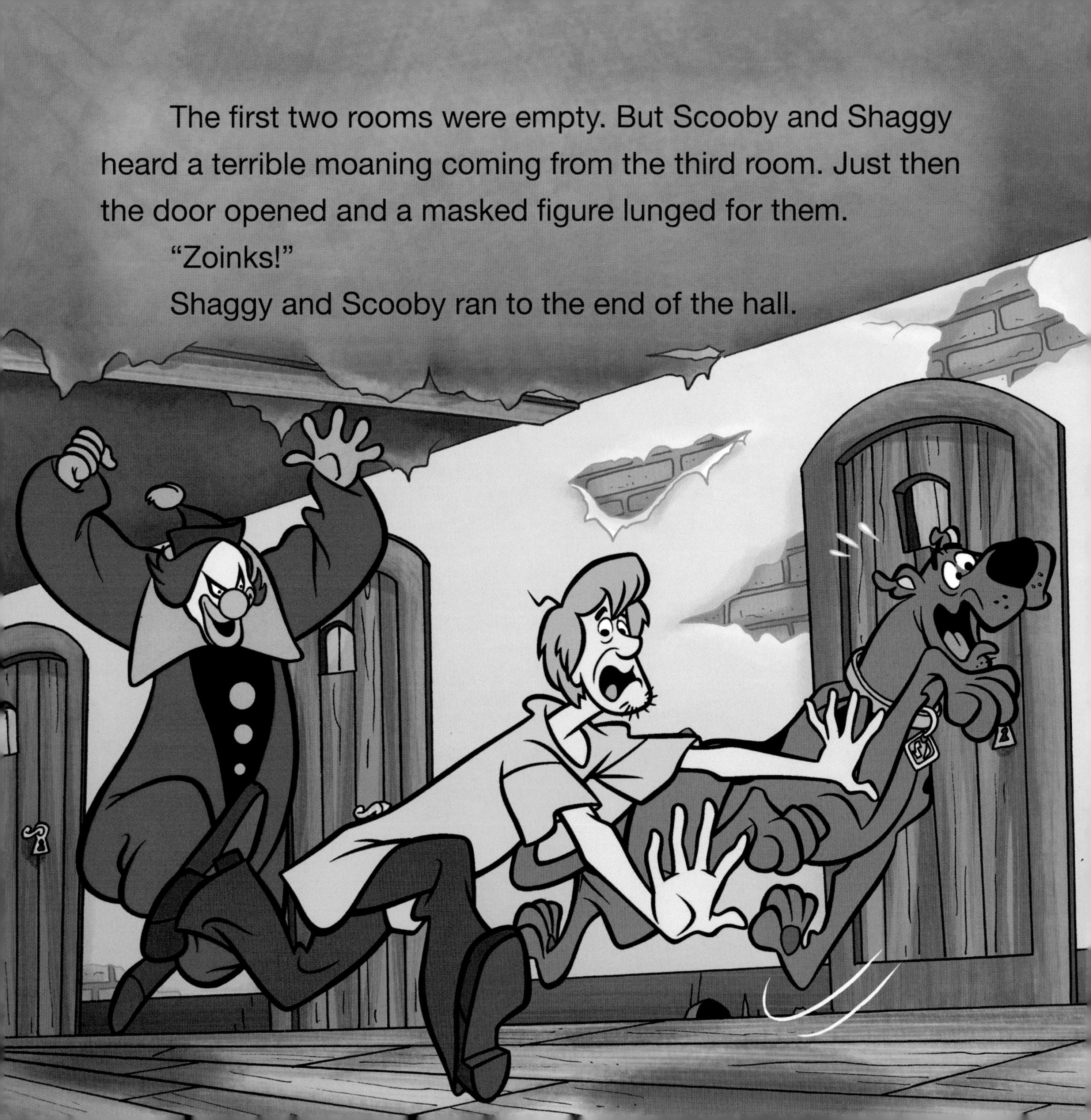

They opened the last door on the left, ran inside, and slammed it shut.

"Like, yikes!" said Shaggy. "That was a close one!"

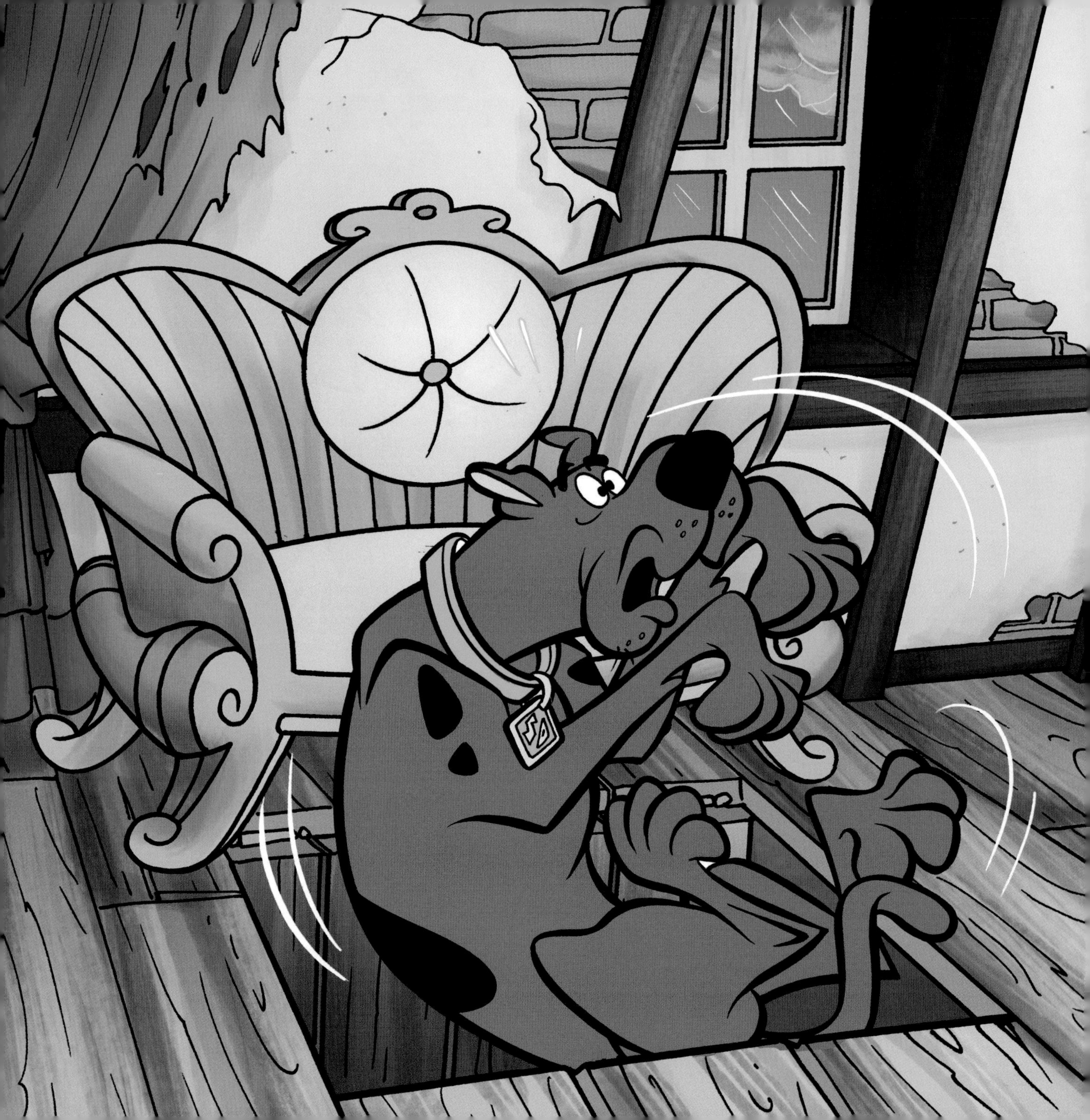

Inside the room, the paint was peeling off the walls and the floorboards were broken. But the room was empty.

"Whew," said Shaggy. "All this searching is making me hungry. I think it's time for a Scooby Snack break."

Scooby eagerly agreed and plopped down on an old-looking chair.

Whump! Scooby was launched from the chair, down through a trapdoor, and onto the floor below!

Luckily, Fred was on the floor below, and Scooby fell right into his arms! Fred wasn't expecting to play catcher, and he lost his balance. He wobbled and fell backward against a bookcase.

Whoosh! The bookcase turned around. Suddenly, Fred and Scooby found themselves inside a secret lab!

Meanwhile, Velma and Daphne checked the area around the front door. The owner was nowhere to be seen, but Velma did spot something on the floor.

"I wonder what this stuff is," Velma said. She bent down and put one finger on the purple goo. It was sticky and squishy. "Let's go find the others and show them," said Daphne.

Daphne and Velma searched for Fred in the library, but they couldn't find him. Suddenly they heard a howl and a "Whoooooaaa!"

Before they knew it, Shaggy fell from the floor above and landed at their feet!

"Shaggy! Are you all right?" asked Daphne.

"Sure, but where's Scooby? One minute we were sitting down for a Scooby Snack, and the next minute he was gone," Shaggy answered.

"Well, you found us instead," said Velma. "Now let's all try to find Fred and Scooby."

The three friends looked around the room for clues. Daphne spotted more of the purple goo seeping from under the bookcase. "Hey guys, look at this!"

Velma noticed that the bookcase had small hinges along one side. "It looks like a secret door. Help me push," she called to the others.

The bookcase spun around revealing Fred and Scooby on the other side.

It also revealed someone else…

It was the hotel owner, Mr. MacDuff—and he was all tied up!
The gang quickly freed him.

"What happened?" Velma asked.

"A masked man grabbed me and took me down here,"
he explained.

Everyone looked around the lab for clues.

In the center of the room was a large hole.

"What's that?" Shaggy said as he peered into the hole.

"That's strange. It's more of that purple goo," began Velma.

"Maybe we can use it to catch the person behind this sticky situation," said Fred.

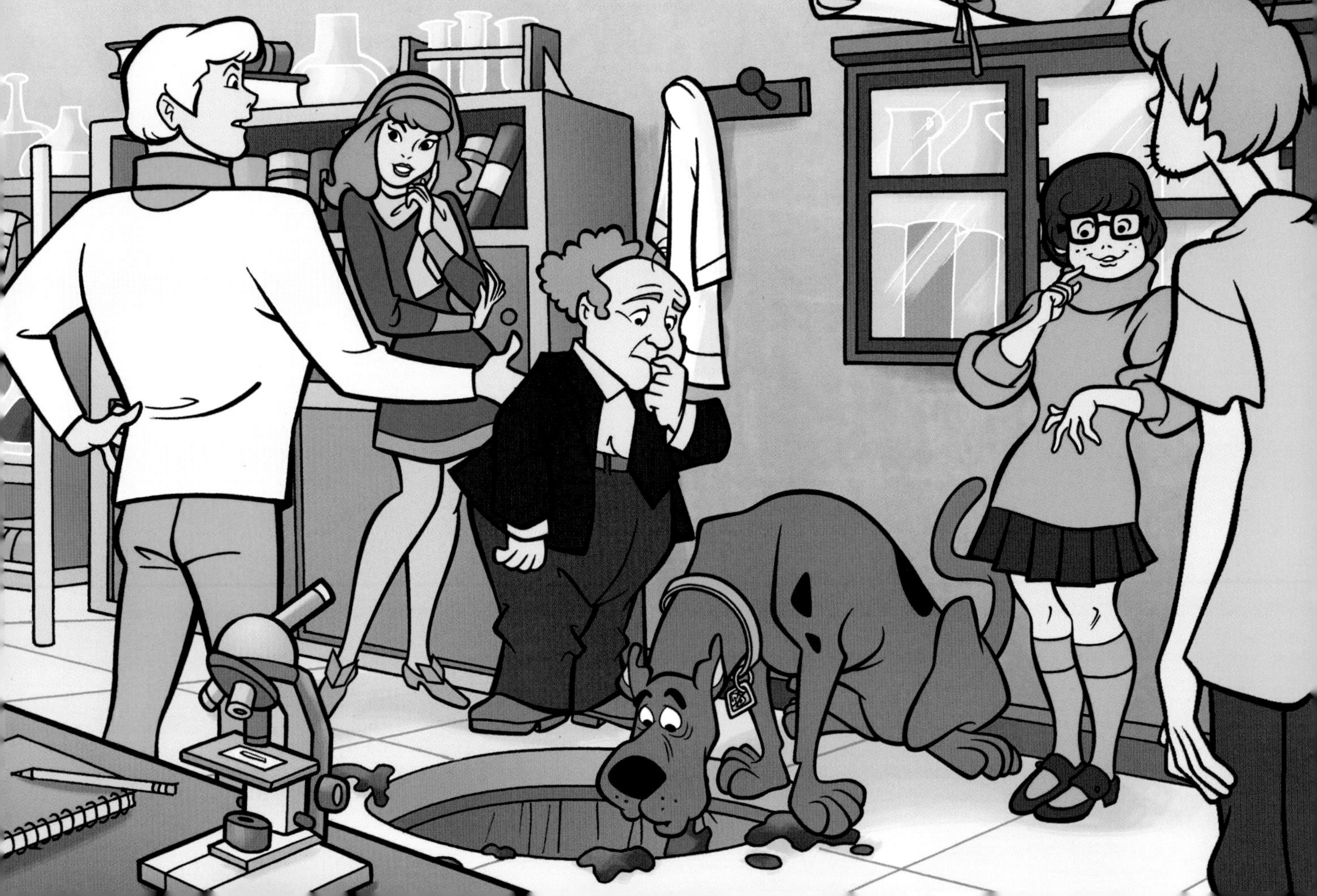

The gang took some of the purple goo from the lab and put it in different parts of the hotel.

Shaggy and Scooby headed back upstairs where they had first heard the moaning. This time, though, they lured out the mysterious stranger with—what else? A Scooby Snack!

According to plan, the masked figure chased Shaggy and Scooby down the hall, out the window, and toward the tower on the roof.

"Now!" yelled Fred.

Purple goo oozed out of the "goo-goyles" on the roof, trapping the masked figure.

"Gotcha!" said Velma.

The gang brought the masked figure—now covered in goo—back inside the hotel. Fred took off the figure's mask, and everyone gasped. It was Marty the bellhop!

"Marty!" exclaimed Mr. MacDuff. "How could you do this to me?"

Marty explained that a rich real estate developer had paid him a lot of money to make everyone think the hotel was haunted. That way, Mr. MacDuff would have to sell the mansion.

"He wanted to tear down the mansion to get to the goo below," explained Marty. "Apparently it's worth a fortune."

Mr. MacDuff was stunned. "I had no idea."

"What will you do with the goo?" Fred asked
Mr. MacDuff.

But before he could answer, Shaggy interrupted. "Like,
I think Scoob has some good ideas!"

"Scooby-Dooby Goo!" exclaimed Scooby,
as everyone laughed.